Beep
and
Bah

James Burks

CAROLRHODA BOOKS • MINNEAPOLIS

FOR ALL THOSE IN SEARCH OF A SOCK. —J.B.

BAH

CAROLRHODA BOOKS
A DIVISION OF LERNER PUBLISHING GROUP, INC.
241 FIRST AVENUE NORTH
MINNEAPOLIS, MN 55401 U.S.A.

WEBSITE ADDRESS: WWW.LERNERBOOKS.COM

LIBRARY OF CONGRESS CATALOGING-IN-PUBLICATION DATA

BURKS, JAMES (JAMES R.)
    BEEP AND BAH / BY JAMES BURKS.
        P.   CM.
    SUMMARY: A ROBOT WHO HUNGERS FOR ADVENTURE AND
    A GOAT WHO WANTS TO AVOID TROUBLE SET OUT TO FIND THE
    MISSING MATE TO A SINGLE SOCK.
        ISBN: 978-0-7613-6567-9 (LIB. BDG. : ALK. PAPER)
        [1. ROBOTS—FICTION. 2. GOATS—FICTION. 3. SOCKS—FICTION.]
    I. TITLE.
    PZ7.B92355BEE 2012
    [E]—DC23   2011018873

MANUFACTURED IN THE UNITED STATES OF AMERICA
1 - PC - 12/31/11

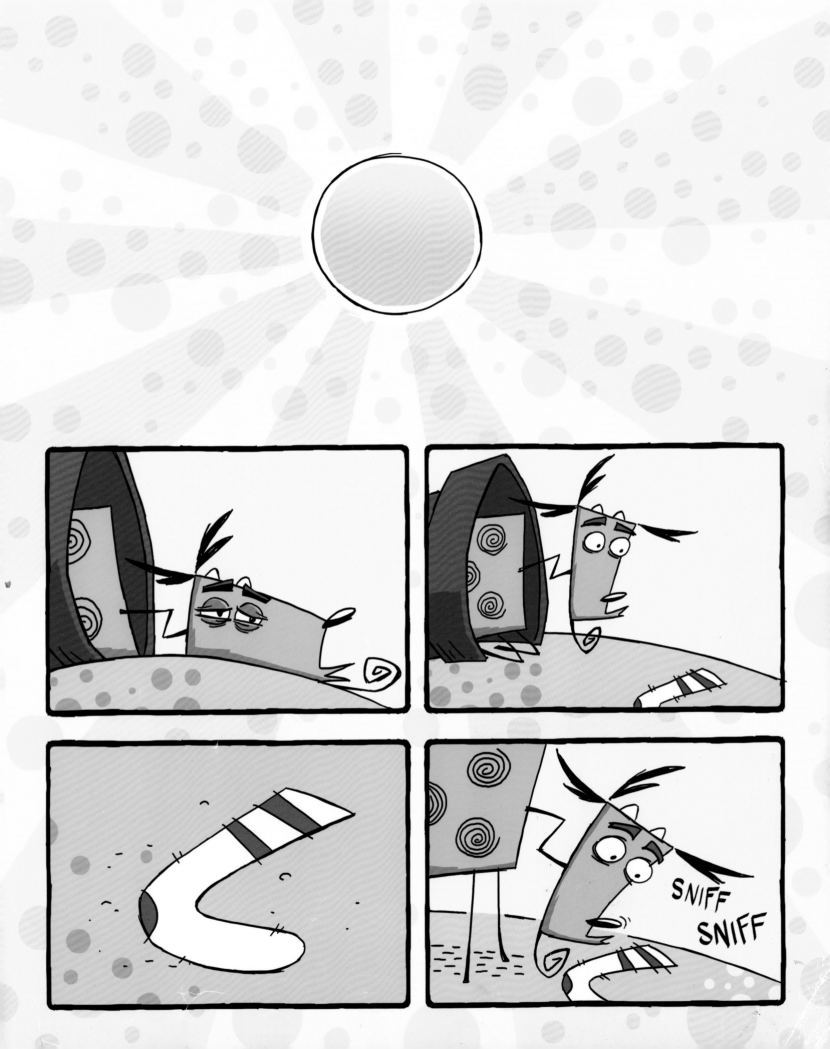

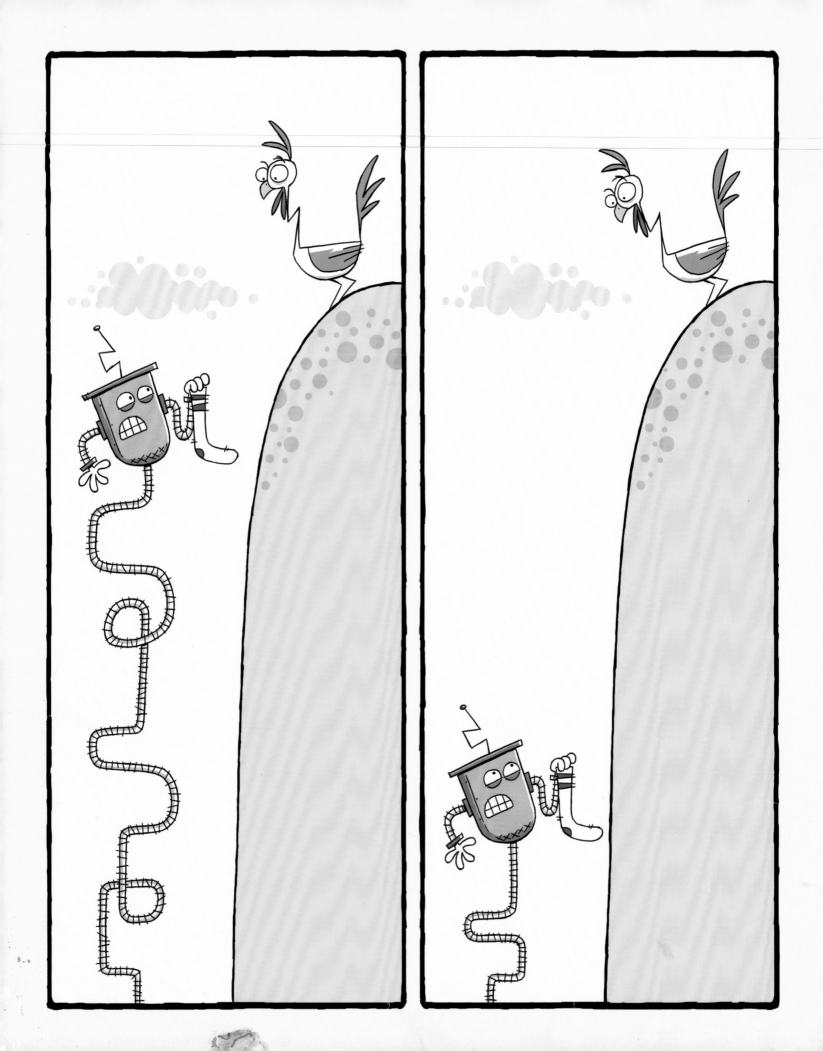

THAT WAS
REFRESHING!

EEEEEEOOOOOOOOOOOOOO!